COWPOKE CLYDE
AND
DIRTY DAWG

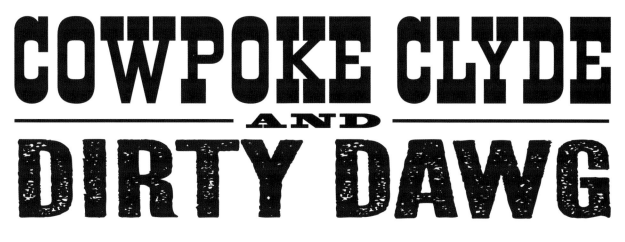

LORI MORTENSEN ILLUSTRATED BY MICHAEL ALLEN AUSTIN

Clarion Books | Houghton Mifflin Harcourt | Boston   New York | 2013

Clarion Books

215 Park Avenue South, New York, New York 10003

Text copyright © 2013 by Lori Mortensen

Illustrations copyright © 2013 by Michael Allen Austin

Clarion Books is an imprint of Houghton Mifflin Harcourt Publishing Company.

www.hmhbooks.com

The text was set in Grandma.

The illustrations were executed in acrylic and colored pencil on Strathmore 500 series illustration board.

Book design by Sharismar Rodriguez

Library of Congress Cataloging-in-Publication Data

Mortensen, Lori, 1955–

Cowpoke Clyde and Dirty Dawg / by Lori Mortensen ; illustrated by Michael Allen Austin.

p. cm.

Summary: Following increasingly chaotic attempts to give his dog a bath, Cowpoke Clyde

discovers there is only one way to get Dawg into the tub.

ISBN 978-0-547-23993-4 (hardcover)

[1. Stories in rhyme. 2. Dogs—Fiction. 3. Baths—Fiction. 4. Cowboys—Fiction.]

I. Austin, Michael, 1965– ill. II. Title.

PZ8.3.M8422Cow 2013

[E]—dc23   2011052429

Manufactured in China

SCP 10 9 8 7 6 5 4 3 2 1

4500396826

For my daughter, Jaimie,
who used to wish she had all
the dogs in the world
—L.M.

For Riley,
who has taught me to face each day
with unrestrained joy
—M.A.A.

COWPOKE CLYDE propped up his feet.
His house was clean, his chores complete.
He'd even washed the kitchen floor
and shooed the horseflies out the door.

Then right behind his cookin' pot,
he spied one thing he'd plumb forgot:
ol' Dawg, his faithful, snorin' friend,
all caked with mud from end to end.

Clyde looked around his tidy shack.
"I'll scrub him down, then come on back,
eat my soup, and take a nap.
Why, washin' Dawg will be a snap."

7

Clyde set his hat and grabbed a rope,
filled some buckets, snatched the soap.
But right before he sprung his plan,
ol' Dawg woke up, and off he ran.

9

Spillin' all the black bean soup.
Shootin' through the chicken coop.
Chickens, fur, and feathers flew,
stirrin' up a filthy brew.

"Gadzooks!" yelled Clyde. "This ain't no joke.

Come back here, boy, and get yer soak!"

But Dawg ignored his mighty pleas.

Instead Dawg left a trail of . . .

FLEAS!

Pesky fleas that jumped and bit.
Fleas that caused a scratchin' fit.

Clyde called to Dawg, "Don't run away!
Come get yer bath, and *then* we'll play."

Dawg paid no mind. So with a cry,
Clyde swung his rope and let it fly
straight at that ornery, dirty Dawg—
but missed his mark and roped a . . .

HOG!

A hog so big it snapped the rope.
A hog that skittered in the soap.

Soon chickens, fleas, and one fat hog
were gettin' soaked instead of Dawg.

Clyde curled his lips and set his brow.
He'd get that Dawg someway, somehow.
"Come on now, boy," he called real sweet.
"Come here and get yer favorite treat!

"I got a bone! Some jerky, too.
Smell it? See? It's just fer you!"
Dawg sniffed the air across the flats.
But 'stead of Dawg, Clyde got six . . .

CATS!

Six cats that hissed and fluffed their tails.
Six cats that toppled soapy pails.

Now chickens, fleas, six cats, a hog
were gettin' soaked instead of Dawg.

Clyde came up with the perfect trick.
He climbed aboard his wagon quick.
"*This* will fool ol' Dawg," he cried.
"Get up now, boy! Let's take a ride."

Dawg circled 'round and twitched an ear.
Clyde bode his time till Dawg came near.
Then just like some pathetic fool,
Clyde sneezed and startled his ol' . . .

MULE!

A mule that brayed and broke the hitch.
A mule that kicked Clyde in a ditch.

Now chickens, cats, a mule, a hog
were gettin' soaked instead of Dawg.

Clyde cursed the mule, tucked in his shirt,
wiped off feathers, fur, and dirt.
"Fine!" he yelled. "I don't care none!"
He kicked a pail. Ol' Dawg had won.

Clyde shooed the chickens, cats, and hog
and swore one day he'd get that Dawg.
That's when it hit him like a joke.
"Forget it, Dawg! *I'll* take a soak!"

He cleared the mess and grabbed some grub,
heated water, filled the tub.
Then, soakin' sweet beneath the moon,
he warbled out a cowpoke tune.

A tune that rattled like a snake.
A tune that set the stars to shake.

Then lightnin' quick, a howlin' sound
split the night and shook the ground.
And with an awful splash Clyde knew
he warn't alone. Now there was . . .

TWO!

Two that soaked beneath the moon.

Two that liked to howl and croon.

And ever since that fateful night,
Cowpoke Clyde and Dawg don't fight.
'Cause when they're filthy head to toe

Clyde and Dawg know where to go.